W9-CHI-501

Dear Parent:

Congratulations! Your child is taking the first steps on an exciting journey. The destination? Independent reading!

STEP INTO READING® will help your child get there. The program offers books at five levels that accompany children from their first attempts at reading to reading success. Each step includes fun stories, fiction and nonfiction, and colorful art. There are also Step into Reading Sticker Books, Step into Reading Math Readers, and Step into Reading Phonics Readers— a complete literacy program with something to interest every child.

Learning to Read, Step by Step!

Ready to Read Preschool–Kindergarten
• big type and easy words • rhyme and rhythm • picture clues
For children who know the alphabet and are eager to begin reading.

Reading with Help Preschool–Grade 1
• basic vocabulary • short sentences • simple stories
For children who recognize familiar words and sound out new words with help.

Reading on Your Own Grades 1–3
• engaging characters • easy-to-follow plots • popular topics
For children who are ready to read on their own.

Reading Paragraphs Grades 2–3
• challenging vocabulary • short paragraphs • exciting stories
For newly independent readers who read simple sentences with confidence.

Ready for Chapters Grades 2–4
• chapters • longer paragraphs • full-color art
For children who want to take the plunge into chapter books but still like colorful pictures.

STEP INTO READING® is designed to give every child a successful reading experience. The grade levels are only guides. Children can progress through the steps at their own speed, developing confidence in their reading, no matter what their grade.

Remember, a lifetime love of reading starts with a single step!

For Fran, who had an alligator but no pony
—A.P.S.

Copyright © 2003 Disney Enterprises, Inc. All rights reserved under International and Pan-American Copyright Conventions. Published in the United States by Random House Children's Books, a division of Random House, Inc., New York, and simultaneously in Canada by Random House of Canada Limited, Toronto, in conjunction with Disney Enterprises, Inc.

www.stepintoreading.com

Educators and librarians, for a variety of teaching tools, visit us at www.randomhouse.com/teachers

Library of Congress Cataloging-in-Publication Data
Posner-Sanchez, Andrea.
A pony for a princess / by Andrea Posner-Sanchez ; illustrated by Francesc Mateu.
    p.   cm. — (Step into reading. A step 2 book)
SUMMARY: Belle uses sugar cubes to befriend a wild pony.
ISBN 0-7364-2045-2 (pbk.) — ISBN 0-7364-8016-1 (lib. bdg.)
[1. Ponies—Fiction.]
I. Mateu, Francesc, ill.   II. Title.   III. Series: Step into reading. Step 2 book.
PZ7.P83843 Po 2003   [E]—dc21   2002015453

Printed in the United States of America   11 10 9 8 7 6 5 4 3 2

STEP INTO READING, RANDOM HOUSE, and the Random House colophon are registered trademarks of Random House, Inc.

STEP INTO READING®

STEP 2

♦ P R I N C E S S

A Pony
for a
Princess

By Andrea Posner-Sanchez

Illustrated by Francesc Mateu

Random House 🏠 New York

Belle picked out a book
from the castle library.

Then she looked
out the window.

The sun was shining.

"I think I will read
outside today," she said.

Belle left the castle.

She walked past the barn.

There was a big
pile of hay
by the barn.

She walked past
the apple tree.
There was a big
basket of apples
under the tree.

Belle sat down to read.

Belle read and read.
Before long,
she felt hungry.

Belle put down her book.
She walked back
to the castle
to get some lunch.

Belle put a sandwich,
some lemonade,
and some sugar cubes
into a picnic basket.

"And I will pick
    an apple for dessert,"
she said.

Belle went back outside.

She walked past the barn.

The hay was gone!

"That is odd," Belle said.

She walked past
the apple tree.
The basket was empty!

"Who could have
eaten all the apples?"
Belle asked.

Belle looked this way.

Belle looked that way.

Then she saw something
behind a bush.
It was a wild pony!

Belle stepped closer.

But the pony was scared.

It ran this way . . .

. . . and it ran that way.
But the pony would not
come to Belle.

Belle had an idea.

She took the sugar cubes

from the picnic basket.

She placed them in a row

on the grass.

Then she stepped back.

The pony ate one
sugar cube.

Then it ate another.
And another.

Soon the pony was

right next to Belle!

Belle held out the
last sugar cube.
The pony ate it right
from her hand!

She reached out to pat

the pony's soft nose.

Belle was happy.
She led the pretty pony
to the barn.

And before long,
the princess and
the pony became
great friends.